BRAVE LIKE JACK

WRITTEN BY: MARISSA CUNNYNGHAM
ILLUSTRATED BY: AYAN MANSOORI

DEDICATION

This book was inspired by my son Jack, who dealt with anxiety. This book is for you, son. I want to start out by thanking my husband and family for always cheering me on to pursue my dream of becoming an author. I want to thank my friends Landry Angel, Emily Nance, and Karley Stafford for reading every manuscript to this book and encouraging me along the way. I want to thank my editor Chelsea Tornetto for helping me portray this story. I want to thank my illustrator Ayan Mansoori for bringing my story to life. I want to thank Author Michelle Bradley for helping me on this self-publishing journey. I couldn't do this without all of you. Most importantly, I want to thank God for giving me this passion that he instilled in my heart and using it to impact others.

My name is Jack Sawyer.
Mama said it's a good, strong name! But, yesterday, I didn't feel strong on my way to school. I felt scared.

MAMA BUCKLED ME INTO MY SEAT, AND I STARTED TO CRY.
SHE HELD MY HAND AND SAID, "CLOSE YOUR EYES AND SAY THIS PRAYER,
DARLING. WITH THE HELP OF YOU GOD, I CAN!"

I CLOSED MY EYES AND REPEATED, "WITH THE HELP OF YOU GOD, I CAN." I FOUGHT BACK MY TEARS AND SMILED AT HER.

MAMA DROPPED ME OFF AT SCHOOL, AND AFTER AN HOUR OR TWO, I STARTED TO MISS HER. IT FELT LIKE A BUNCH OF BUTTERFLIES WERE IN MY TUMMY. I JUST WANTED TO GO HOME. MY TEACHERS TOLD ME EVERYTHING WAS GOING TO BE OKAY, BUT IT DIDN'T FEEL THAT WAY.

MAMA'S PRAYER COULD'VE HELPED ME, BUT I COULD ONLY REMEMBER "WITH
THE HELP..." AND I FORGOT THE REST. WITH THE HELP OF WHAT? OR WHO?
I WISH I COULD REMEMBER! MY FRIENDS TRIED TALKING TO ME, BUT I JUST
SHRUGGED MY SHOULDERS.

MAMA PICKED ME UP FROM SCHOOL, AND I KNOW SHE COULD TELL THAT I HAD A ROUGH DAY. "DID YOU REMEMBER THE PRAYER?" MAMA ASKED.

"I REALLY REALLY TRIED HARD TO REMEMBER, BUT I JUST COULDN'T."
"THAT'S OKAY! MAYBE NEXT TIME, BABY." MAMA HUGGED ME.

I PLAYED BASEBALL AT HOME WITH DAD. WE HAD SO MUCH FUN! BUT THAT NIGHT WAS MY FIRST BASEBALL PRACTICE WITH MY FRIENDS. WE GOT ONTO THE FIELD AND EVERYONE LINED UP TO BAT.

THAT FEELING CAME AGAIN. THE SCARY ONE. THE ONE THAT SAID, "YOU CAN'T DO THIS!" THE LINE WAS GETTING SHORTER. IT WAS ALMOST MY TURN TO BAT. MY TUMMY STARTED TO HURT. I TRIED TO REMEMBER THE PRAYER, BUT I WAS TOO NERVOUS TO REMEMBER.

EVERYONE WAS WATCHING. ALL EYES WERE ON ME. JUST ONE MORE PLAYER, THEN IT WAS MY TURN. "JACK, YOU'RE UP!" THE COACH CALLED. MY FRIENDS WERE CHEERING, "YOU CAN DO IT, JACK!"

I WALKED UP SLOWLY TO THE PLATE, BUT I STARTED TO CRY JUST BEFORE I GOT THERE. I RAN AWAY FROM THE FIELD INTO THE BLEACHERS WHERE MY MAMA SAT. "I CAN'T DO IT, MAMA," I SAID, AS TEARS ROLLED DOWN MY CHEEKS.

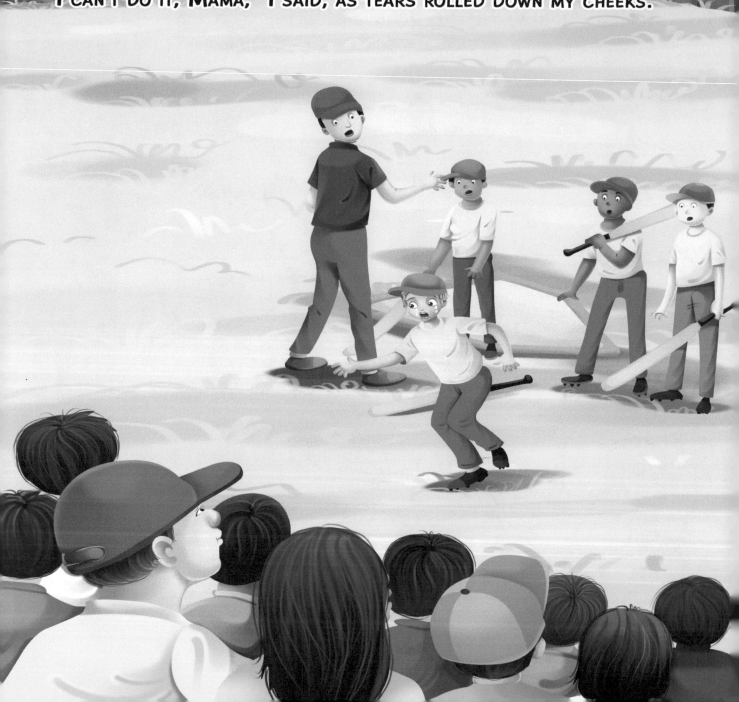

She wrapped her arm around me and said, "Jack, remember, 'With the help of you God, I can.'" "I tried to remember it, Mama, but I was too scared." "You will remember, baby, exactly when you need it," said Mama.

MY FRIENDS FOUND ME AFTER PRACTICE, AND THEY GAVE ME A BIG BEAR HUG
MY BEST FRIEND, JUDD, WHISPERED, "I WAS SCARED TOO. IT'S OKAY!" WE
PLAYED HIDE-N-SEEK UNTIL OUR PARENTS MADE US GO HOME.

MAMA REMINDED ME IT'S MY COUSIN COLT'S BIRTHDAY PARTY TODAY. HE'S HAVING AN OBSTACLE COURSE! THERE WILL BE A LOT OF KIDS THERE. HOPEFULLY, I WILL NOT BE AFRAID.

WE SHOWED UP AT THE PARTY, AND I SAW ALL THE KIDS PLAYING IN THE OBSTACLES. MAMA SAID, "GO PLAY AND HAVE FUN!" BUT I WAS STILL TOO SCARED! MY BROTHER AND SISTER WERE PLAYING, BUT I DIDN'T LEAVE MAMA'S SIDE.

I WISH I WASN'T SCARED. I WISH I COULD BE BRAVE. MAYBE I CAN...WITH SOME HELP! I CLOSED MY EYES AND PRAYED TO MYSELF, "WITH THE HELP OF YOU GOD, I CAN." I SMILED SO BIG AND DID A HAPPY DANCE BECAUSE I FINALLY REMEMBERED THE PRAYER WITHOUT MAMA'S HELP.

JUST THEN, I NOTICED A GIRL WHO WAS HANGING ONTO HER MAMA'S LEG TOO
I RAN UP TO HER AND WHISPERED, "IT'S OKAY TO FEEL SCARED. I DO TOO!"
BUT TOGETHER, WITH THIS PRAYER, WE CAN BE AS BRAVE AS SUPERHEROES!

Until we were shouting it from the rooftops, "WITH THE HELP OF YOU GOD, I CAN!"

It made us laugh so hard that we forgot we were ever even scared. My new friend and I played on the obstacle course all afternoon. We had fun! And most importantly, I learned that even when it feels impossible to be brave...

"WITH THE HELP OF YOU GOD, I CAN."

Letter to Parent of an Anxious Child

To all the parents out there with an anxious child, I know what you're going through. I want you to know you're not alone. I know it's tough and frustrating, but hang in there. It gets better, I promise. They all bloom in their own time, when they decide they're ready. I knew Jack would come out of his shell when he was ready and his time may have not been ours, but he eventually got there. The hardest part of having an anxious child was I truly wanted everyone to see Jack the way I saw him. The intelligent, playful, and silly loving boy that I know. It absolutely broke my heart when I knew his teachers and friends didn't see him that way because he was too shy to talk, too shy to play with friends, or even too shy to do anything but keep to himself. But he showed up and for Jack that is a huge step in the right direction. We simply cannot force our children to talk, we cannot force them to play a sport, and we honestly cannot force them to do anything. All we can do is guide them and help them along the way. Here are some scriptures to help instill into your child's heart, because nothing is better than God's word to reassure them when they need it the most!

Scriptures to help the anxious hearted child

"Don't be afraid, for I am with you. Don't be discouraged, for I am your God. I will strengthen you and help you." Isaiah 41:10 NLT

"For I hold you by your right hand __ I, the LORD your God. And I say to you, "Don't be afraid. I am here to help you." Isaiah 41:13 NLT

"The Lord is my rock, my fortress, and my savior; my God is my rock, in whom I find protection. He is my shield, the power that saves me, and my place of safety." Psalms 18:2 NLT

"Give all your worries and cares to God, for he cares about you."
1 Peter 5:7 NLT

"For God has not given us a spirit of fear and timidity, but of power, love, and self-discipline." 2 Timothy 1:7 NLT

"What's more, I am with you, and I will protect you wherever you go."
Genesis 28:15 NLT

"When I am afraid, I put my trust in you." Psalms 56:3 NLT

"I love you, LORD; you are my strength." Psalms 18:1 NLT

CPSIA information can be obtained
at www.ICGtesting.com
Printed in the USA
LVHW072317270721
693917LV00005B/214